Patrick's Great Grass Adventure

With Greg the Grass Farmer

Joel Salatin and Rachel Salatin

HEY! THAT'S ME!

Patrick Pigeon noticed some crumbs on the sidewalk and fluttered down to peck them off the hard concrete. His toes clicked and clacked as he walked. The hard surface hurt his beak as he pecked the crumbs. He'd grown up nearby in the steeple of St. Peter Lutheran Church, but yearned for a different place to settle.

Several times a day the steeple's bells clanging and rattling made Patrick Pigeon's head hurt. Sirens, horns, and crowds of people didn't help either.

Patrick Pigeon's confidence and desire to search for a different home sent him swooping over the city. He spotted a green area and soon came to a landing on the grass in a park. It was soft. A passerby came too close and sent Patrick fluttering to the top of a metal lamp post. His toes wrapped around the hard steel.

HONK!

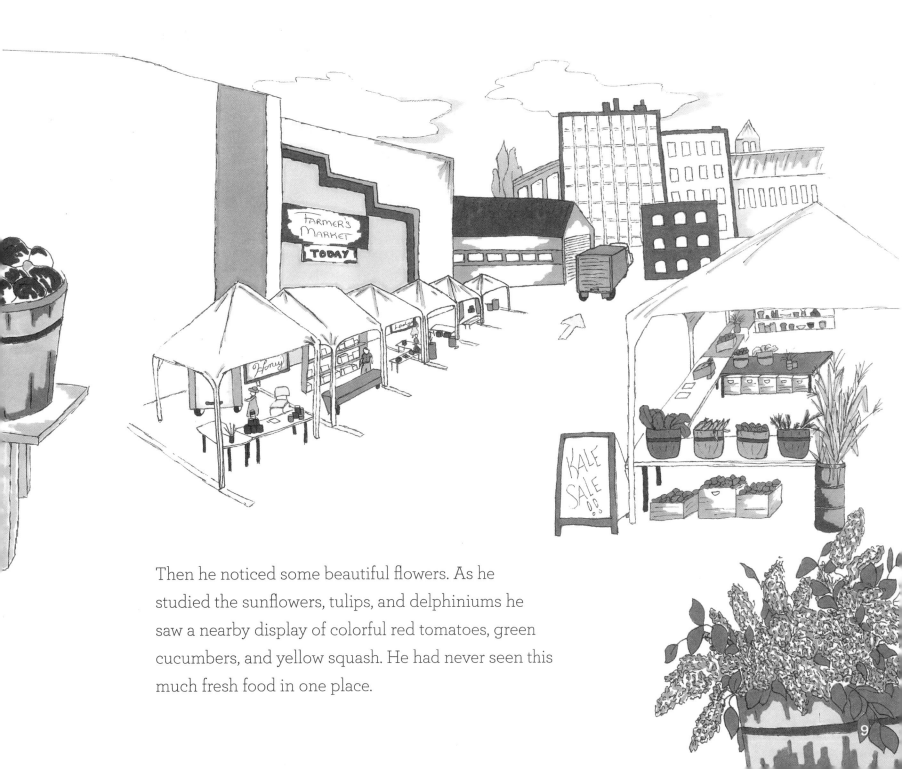

Then he noticed some beautiful flowers. As he studied the sunflowers, tulips, and delphiniums he saw a nearby display of colorful red tomatoes, green cucumbers, and yellow squash. He had never seen this much fresh food in one place.

9

With his keen eyesight, Patrick spotted an interesting character wearing a bow tie and suspenders. Some customers turned the pages of a large picture album on the table. To his surprise and delight, he saw chickens — birds like him — walking around on a carpet of green grass. Having just experienced the park lawn, Patrick wanted to live in a place with that much grass.

WINTER HOOP HOUSE HOME

FREE RANGE EGG LAYERS

CHICKENS MOVED EVERY DAY

ON PASTURE

After waiting awhile, Patrick followed Greg who was headed home after a big morning at the market. Staying high above the yellow truck, Patrick soared out of the city toward the country. What would he find in these new surroundings?

Patrick scanned the horizon for a place that
looked like Greg's pictures, but the grass in the
pastures was short and pale green. He flew past
tall concrete tubes that he later learned were
called silos. Big barns and freshly plowed brown
fields made him wonder if he had made a wise
decision to leave the city.

To Patrick's relief, Greg's yellow truck slowed and over a hill appeared lush green grass, and hundreds of feathered friends! Patrick glided to a landing on the top board of the yard fence, where magnificent seed heads from rustling tall grass — really tall grass — tickled his toes. Never had he seen anything like this.

As he looked into the dense pasture, colorful blossoms and sweet smells filled his head. He hopped off the fence and practically somersaulted into the lush carpet. His feet never hit the ground as soft petals and gentle leaves swallowed him like a bed of feathers. He tilted crazily as he tried to gain his footing.

Busy honeybees zigged and zagged from bloom to bloom. Red clover, white clover, blue chicory blossoms, yellow dandelions and fluffy plantain spires joined with the seed-dripping tree-like grasses in such abundance that Patrick hurt with happiness.

At that moment, Patrick heard a door slam and realized Greg the Grass Farmer might be going somewhere. Patrick rolled over and stood up. He gave a mighty leap, flapped his wings, and hacked his way out of the grass forest.

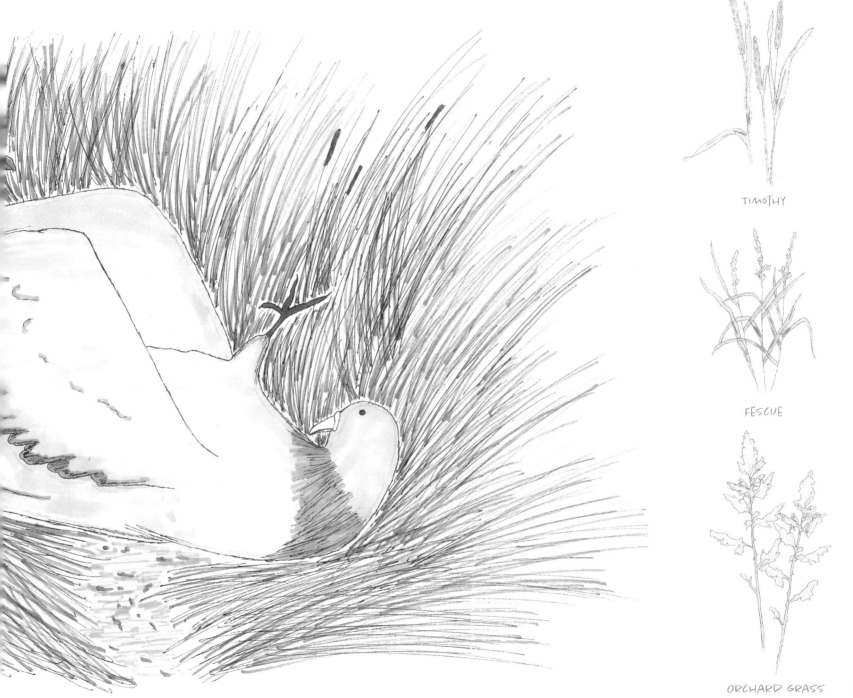

TIMOTHY

FESCUE

ORCHARD GRASS   19

Patrick flew ahead of Greg, and perched in a nearby maple tree. Smoothing down his feathers, he noticed a herd of cows. The grass in their pasture was extremely short, like the grass in the city park.

Greg walked directly to the cows, greeting them with a friendly "hello, ladies," as he approached. The patient cows watched Greg's movements. "Are you hungry?" he asked, good-naturedly.

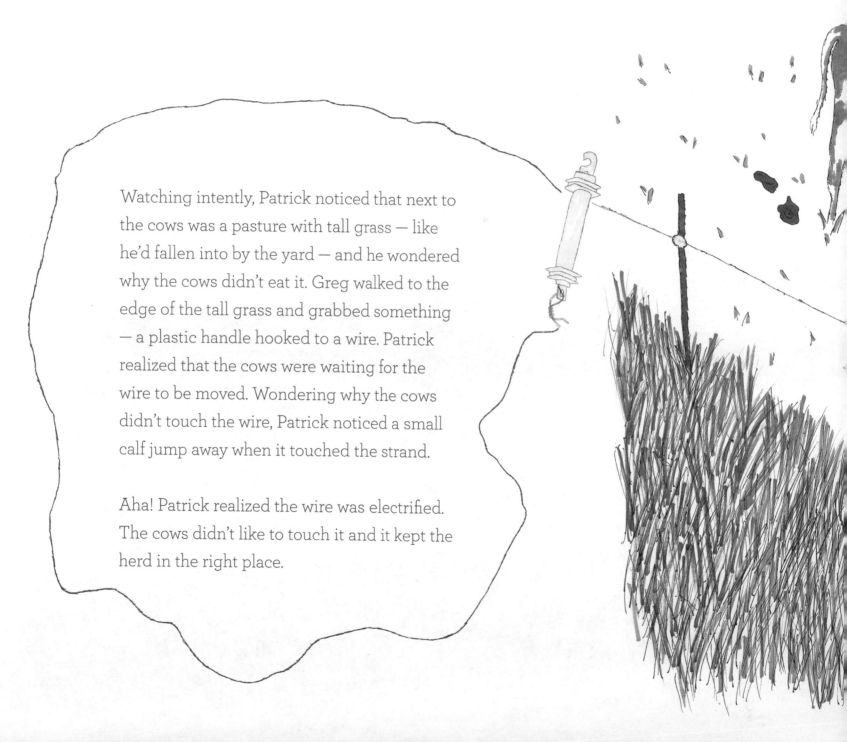

Watching intently, Patrick noticed that next to the cows was a pasture with tall grass — like he'd fallen into by the yard — and he wondered why the cows didn't eat it. Greg walked to the edge of the tall grass and grabbed something — a plastic handle hooked to a wire. Patrick realized that the cows were waiting for the wire to be moved. Wondering why the cows didn't touch the wire, Patrick noticed a small calf jump away when it touched the strand.

Aha! Patrick realized the wire was electrified. The cows didn't like to touch it and it kept the herd in the right place.

ZAP!

CHOMP
CHOMP

MUNCH
MUNCH

"Come on, cows," called Greg. As Greg unhooked the handle and swung open the fence like a long door, the herd flowed into the tall grass, buried muzzles chomping, chewing, nipping and snipping. As the cows grazed across the field, millions of insects jumped out of their grassy hiding places. Patrick noticed tender new grass shoots hiding underneath ready for sunshine and new growth and the dark rich soil supporting them.

Suddenly, Patrick realized grass was far more amazing than a park lawn. It was a grand adventure.

Patrick breathed deeply, enjoying the fresh air cleaned by the fast-growing grass. The herd spread out in the new pasture like buffalo on the prairie. Perhaps the country would be a good place to live after all.

He uncurled his feet from the tree branch and flew down to the pasture where the cows had been moments before. Grasshoppers, crickets, shattered seeds, and grubs were everywhere!

The famished bird feasted. He quickly filled his gizzard with the best tasting treats he'd ever enjoyed. The grass offered a banquet compared to limited sidewalk crumbs.

As the sun set on his day of adventure, Patrick flew up away from the pasture, spied a shed near Greg's house and decided it might offer a good place to rest for the night. His tired wings carried him to the shed, where he nestled into some soft hay. He barely heard the distant sound of a church bell. Snuggling down into the soft nest, Patrick soon fell fast asleep and began dreaming about tomorrow's adventures with Greg the Grass Farmer.

Activity page

Patrick Pigeon sees Greg the Grass Farmer use different tools and work with lots of plants and animals.

Can you find them in the book?

One-hand Sledge Hammer.
It has a short handle, weighs 1 pound, has a large hammer head and is perfect for pounding electric fence stakes into the ground.

Chicory.
It's not a grass, but one of the many tasty and nutritious plants that grows in well-managed pastures. People can eat it in salads when it's young and tender. It produces blue blossoms.

Hay Bales.
Hay is dried grass, like raisins are dried grapes. Greg mows tall grass in early summer, lets it dry in the field, and then bales it into round or square bales. The stored hay ensures plenty of food for the cows in the winter or in a drought when pastures don't produce enough grass.

Mineral Box.
Animals seek minerals to help them get all the nutrition they need to be healthy and grow. Since Greg's farm mimics nature, he gives his cows minerals too.

Solar Panels.
These roof-mounted boxes can turn sunbeams into electricity. Greg's house and shop run on this electrical power.

Raised Garden Beds.
Have you ever grown a carrot or a tomato? Greg not only grows grass; he grows vegetables too. Raised beds are highly productive, especially when he puts composted cow manure on them.

Battery.
This powers Greg's electric fence. As Greg moves the cows around the farm from paddock to paddock, he moves the battery to produce the spark that keeps the cows contained.

Morgan the Cat.
Rachel, this book's illustrator, really likes cats. Morgan is her personal gray kitty who loves being outside catching mice and sleeping in the grass. She also likes to sleep in a basket in the house.

Author

Joel Salatin and his family own and operate Polyface Farm in Virginia's Shenandoah Valley. The farm produces pastured beef, pork, chicken, eggs, turkeys, rabbits, lamb, and ducks, servicing roughly 6,000 families and 50 restaurants in the farm's bio-region. He has written 11 books to date and lectures around the world on land healing, local food systems. He's proud to be Rachel's dad.

Illustrator

Rachel Salatin grew up on Polyface Farm in the Shenandoah Valley of Virginia where she developed a deep appreciation for the land, animals and the work ethic necessary to care for our environment. She received a degree in Interior Design and Business Management and has been working for non-profit art organizations for the past six years. A creative project is always on her drafting table in her home in Staunton, Virginia.